The POKY LITTLE PUPPY

Follows His Nose Home

by Adelaide Holl

illustrated by Alex C. Miclat

GOLDEN PRESS
Western Publishing Company, Inc.
Racine, Wisconsin

G H I J

Five little puppies sat looking out at the lovely grassy meadow beyond their fence.

"Mother," they begged, "may we go over the fence and into the meadow to play?"

"Well," said their mother, "I guess you are getting big enough to see a little of the world. But remember," she cautioned, "stay away from the highway, where there are cars! And be home by dinner time!"

With yips of delight, the puppies tumbled over the
fence and into the meadow.

Their mother added, "Don't get lost! But if you
do, just *sniff* and *sniff* and follow your noses home!"

The four quick little puppies raced along, with the poky little puppy, as usual, tagging behind. They ran and ran, until they came to an apple orchard. A fat pig sat under a tree, chomping juicy, sweet-smelling, rosy apples.

The puppies stared at him. "Are you a car?" asked one puppy.

"Goodness, no!" was the reply. "I'm a pig."

"Then we'll stay and play," said the puppies.

But after a while, one puppy said, "Come on! We want to see more of the world!"

They bounced along in the warm sunshine, until they came to a garden of bright, sweet-smelling flowers. A small brown rabbit sat nibbling tasty clover blossoms.

One puppy spoke up. "You aren't a car, are you?"

"Oh, my, no!" was the reply. "I'm a rabbit."

The puppies stayed to roll in the grass and chase butterflies. Finally they said, "We have seen only a little of the world." So off they raced, up hills and down hills, until they came to a barnyard. There stood a cow eating fresh, sweet hay.

"Are you by any chance a car?" one puppy asked.

"Certainly not!" was the reply. "I'm a cow."

The puppies stopped for a while to chase flies and roll in the mud. Then they bounded off, calling, "There's still more of the world to see!"

They traveled across a field, past a woods, up a hill, and down again. At last they came to a place where there were tall buildings and things racing by making a great noise. ZOOM! SCREECH! HONK, HONK!

They looked in amazement. "What in the world are those things?" they asked one another.

A pigeon was pecking at crumbs on the sidewalk. "Those are cars," said the pigeon.

"Cars!" shouted the puppies all together. "Our mother told us to stay away from cars!"

"Well, then, stay away from the city," advised the pigeon. "The city is filled with cars."

"We must go home at once," said the scared little
puppies. "We must *sniff* and *sniff* and follow our noses
right back."

They sat and sniffed. One puppy said, "I smell the
apple orchard. Follow me!"

Away they ran, following the scent of juicy apples. But they didn't find the apple orchard—just a mound of shiny apples, heaped high at a fruit stand.

A man waved a broom at them and shouted, "Get out of here!"

The frightened little puppies ran till they were quite out of breath. Then they sat down to sniff again.

One puppy said, "I smell the flower garden. Follow
me! Hurry!"

Around the nearest corner they went, sniffing
the fragrance of flowers. But there was no flower
garden—just a lady with a flower cart.

She waved a newspaper and cried, "Go away!"

The puppies ran and ran until their short little legs
were tired. Then they stopped to sniff some more.

One puppy said, "I smell the barnyard. Follow me!"

Off they bounded, following their noses, until they came to a big place where there were many animals. The animals were all locked up behind bars.

A man called to the puppies, "Run along! The zoo is no place for you!"

DON'T
FEED THE
ANIMALS

The puppies ran, with their hearts pounding. At last they had to stop and rest.

"We're lost," said one puppy sadly. "We'll never find our way home."

The poky little puppy spoke up. "I know I'm poky, but I have a very keen puppy nose. I smell puppy footprints—*our* footprints! Follow me!"

He started off, not very fast but very carefully, with his nose to the ground. The other puppies eagerly tagged behind.

Sniff, sniff! He led them up hills and down hills. He led them past the cow in the barnyard.

Sniff, sniff! He led them across a big field. He led them past the rabbit in the flower garden.

Sniff, sniff! He led them alongside a little woods. He led them past the pig in the apple orchard.

Sniff, sniff! He went along, and he went along, through the grassy meadow and all the way back home again!

With little yips of delight, the five little puppies tumbled back over the fence, very tired and out of breath—and very happy.

"We have seen quite a lot of the world," they said to their mother.

"Well, welcome home!" she greeted them. "You're just in time for dinner!"